Why Table Tennis?

10 Aspects of the Sport that Will Change Your Life

Written By Jacob Boyd, Samson Dubina, and Sarah Jalli

©2020
v05-01-2020

On the Front Cover: Coach Samson Dubina

Front Cover Photo Credit: Seth Pech
Back Cover Photo Credits: Chris Jordan and Mike Boyd
Inside Photo Credit: Chris Jordan and Seth Pech and Bridgestone
Bible Quote: NKJV

Editor: Larry Hodges
Cover Design by Simplex Creative

Table of Contents

Table Tennis Facts

- Olympic Sport Since 1988
- Rapidly Gaining in Popularity in the US
- 300 Million Players Worldwide
- 600 Million Fans Worldwide
- Most Popular Indoor Sport in the World
- Second Most Popular Sport Overall
- Ball Speed is 173 Hits/Minute - that's almost 3 per second!
- Maximum Spin is 8000 RPMs
- Burn up to 500 Calories Per Match for Olympic Level Players
- Current World Record is 32,000 Hits in a Single Rally
- Domestic and International College Scholarships Available
- Find a Club Near YOU - Table Tennis Clubs in All Major US Cities

Introduction

By Samson Dubina

The Olympic sport of table tennis is well-respected worldwide for the dexterity of the athletes, the speed of the rallies, and the excitement of watching players of all ages and nationalities compete for world titles. Here in the US, very little is known about table tennis ... Until Now! *Why Table Tennis* takes you on a one-hour journey where you will explore the vastness of the sport, understand how it is healthy for the mind and body, how it has impacted world history, and why it can impact your life too!!!

Buckle up for this one-hour journey...
The Olympic Sport of Table Tennis!

Chapter 1

Table Tennis vs Ping Pong

Ping Pong and Table Tennis are two separate sports. There is a ping pong world championship played with sandpaper paddles and there is a table tennis world championship played by Olympians using carbon fiber rackets and explosive rubber. Both of these sports have different rules, different equipment, different scoring, different uniforms, different balls, and are played by two different types of people.

In this first chapter, we are going to describe why a large percentage of the US population loves to play recreational ping pong. In the following chapters, we are going to lay out why we believe the Olympic sport of table tennis is the BEST sport in the world.

Recreational ping pong is a fun game for the whole family – young kids, teens, adults, seniors, grandparents, and even great-grandparents can enjoy playing one-on-one, doubles, or teams! This family pastime is now rapidly gaining momentum in professional circuits and recreational circles worldwide, with 300 million players, according to Pledge Sports USA. As recreational ping pong continues to grow here in the US, our hope is that many players come to know the sport that we love and cherish so much ... The Olympic Sport of Table Tennis.

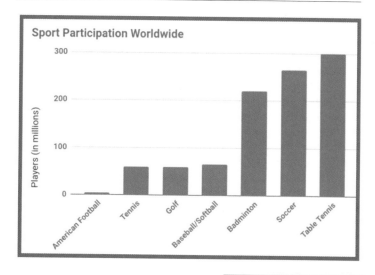

Sport Participation Worldwide

"I started playing recreationally when I was six years old. Our family was going on a cruise to the Bahamas and it was advertised as having a ping pong tournament! YAY! My mom said that if I played every day, she would let me enter the tournament. Well, there was no tournament on the cruise, but it increased my interest level and I played recreational ping pong almost every day with my parents and relatives. At age 12, I was introduced to the Olympic sport of table tennis, which opened up my eyes to a whole new world and furthered my daily fun and challenges!"

Testimonial by Samson Dubina

Chapter 2
Healthy for the Body

Regardless if you are just learning table tennis or you are a contender for the US Olympic Team, you can be sure of one thing, table tennis is healthy for the body. It is really a FULL-BODY WORKOUT involving the arms, legs, chest, back, hips, and core muscles! According to Science of Table Tennis (by Ultimate Table Tennis), 80% of the muscles are in play below the neck region.

Olympic athletes practice an average of six hours per day! In addition to training on the table, Olympians do daily strength, speed, flexibility, coordination, and reflex training. So why does the body need to be so well-conditioned? Great question! Because top players need to be able to generate amazing racket speeds to produce speed and spin while still being quick enough to return balls coming from only nine feet away. How fast is it? Let's do a comparison to other sports.

- **When returning a soccer kick from 12 yards away, you have 0.7 seconds to react.**
- **When returning the world's fastest baseball pitch, you have 0.375 seconds to react.**
- **When returning the world's fastest tennis serve, you have 0.325 seconds to react.**
- **The average blink of an eye is 0.3 seconds.**
- **According to ESPN Sports Science, when returning a professional table tennis hit, you have 0.11 seconds to react. Wow! That is fast!**

REACTION TIME

With only 0.11 seconds to react, professional players need to be in world-class condition. Also, it isn't just one hit but dozens of very fast balls blazing at you and spinning at a rate of 8000 RPMs from only nine feet away!

Is it all about quick reflexes and wrist action? No! There is plenty of footwork involved as well. A professional table tennis court is 46' x 23' and the players cover every square inch of it – looping, smashing, chopping, and lobbing. So how much movement goes on? According to Science of Table Tennis (by Ultimate Table Tennis), the average table tennis player travels a distance of 2.49 miles per match at the Olympic level!

Testimonial by Sarah Jalli

"As a member of the US National Team, my fitness routine includes exercises for speed, such as agility ladder and short distance sprints, exercises for strength such as weight training, exercises for endurance like high intensity interval sprints, and I also implement exercises to improve my flexibility and mobility."

Testimonial by Samson Dubina

"I trained professionally with the Canadian Olympic table tennis team for three years. After retiring from professional table tennis playing, I had to make a decision between full-time coaching vs my original plan of becoming a full-time firefighter-paramedic. I took the firefighter fitness challenge and finished in first place, beating all the other firefighters in speed, strength, agility, and balance workouts! Yes, table tennis does have a significant impact on your fitness level!"

So what about you?

- Maybe you aren't an elite-athlete-type-person…
- Maybe you are just starting the sport…
- Will you get a good workout?

In a recent study by Home Leisure Direct, they found that table tennis improves your life in 29 different ways. Some of the physical benefits include improved reflexes, improved blood flow, cardiovascular health, balance, flexibility, joint health, explosive strength, and it is also a great form of stress relief.

Regardless if you want to win an Olympic Gold Medal or not, fitness should be part of your life. What job do you have? Is it a physical job like a firefighter or construction worker? Table tennis can help! Is it a non-physical job like an accountant or librarian? Table tennis can help no matter what your profession! Part of being healthy is staying fit and table tennis is the best fit for that.

Testimonial by Ron Rozumulski

"I stood on my scale and it read – ONE AT A TIME PLEASE! I knew it was time to lose weight. Since then, I lost nearly 50 pounds playing the sport of table tennis. I decided to quit being a couch potato and become more active. Table tennis (and a better diet) helped me achieve this weight loss. The Samson Dubina Table Tennis Academy helped me with this goal. Abstaining from most sugar products and participating in lessons, classes, leagues, and club play was instrumental in my weight loss."

Chapter 3
Healthy for the Mind

T able tennis is healthy for the minds of children, teens, college students, working adults, and senior citizens. Scientists now believe that table tennis is the #1 BRAIN SPORT as it enhances brain function, unlike any other sport. According to Dr. Wendy Suzuki, Professor of Neuroscience and Psychology at New York University, and Dr. Daniel Amen, Clinical Neuroscientist and Psychiatrist, table tennis enhances motor functions, strategy functions, and long-term memory functions. Studies show that up to five parts of the brain can be stimulated simultaneously while playing table tennis. These include:

- Primary Motor Cortex - responsible for balance, motor movements, and hand-eye coordination
- Prefrontal Cortex - responsible for strategic planning and decision making
- Frontal Temporal Lobe - responsible for controlling focus, concentration, decision making, and problem-solving
- Hippocampus - responsible for retaining long-term information
- Basal Ganglia - responsible for maintaining composure

Two recent studies showing the effectiveness of table tennis on the human brain include "The Effect of Table Tennis Practice on Mental Ability" (Kawano M.M., Mimura K., Kenoko M.), and "Effects of Physical Exercise Intervention on Motor Skills and Executive Functions in Children with ADHD" (Pan C.Y., Tsai C.L., Chu C.H., Sung M.C., Huang C.Y., Ma W.Y.). These studies concluded that regular table tennis training can help maintain mental capacity and prevent or delay senile dementia in addition to providing a therapeutic alternative to medication for children with attention deficit hyperactivity disorder (ADHD), autism, and mild mental disabilities. It has been scientifically proven that if you play table tennis for 10 minutes a day, it boosts activity in the prefrontal cortex and cerebellum. A study of 164 Korean women aged 60 and over showed that table tennis improved more brain function than dancing, walking, gymnastics, or resistant training.

Other studies have shown that table tennis can also improve the dynamic visual activity (ability to see objects when you are moving fast) of the general population, the biomotor capacities (strength, endurance, speed, flexibility, and balance/coordination) of children in general, and the static balance (ability to maintain equilibrium when stationary) of deaf children. Table tennis also triggers the increase of neurotransmitters in the brain, which can help reduce depression and stress while improving memory and moods. Many parents complain about their children having short attention spans or lack of focus, which can lead to poor performance in school. Table tennis is a sport that emphasizes extreme focusing skills that can help improve schoolwork and long-term skills that are healthy for the mind. The repetitive approach to practice and drills requires that players become experts in the maneuvers and tactics that they've learned, which is also teaching life-long skills in memory and work ethic.

When Sarah Jalli first started playing table tennis, she wore glasses. After just a year of training, her eyes dramatically improved and she now sees 20/20 without glasses. Fiona Dubina is having similar benefits for her eyes. She currently has strabismus (cross-eyed) and she can't see depth; everything looks 2D instead of 3D like most of us. With daily table tennis training, she is now beginning to see depth. Fiona is using table tennis training as one of her primary means of improving her eyesight.

There are many aspects to why table tennis is good for the mind, but one of the best is that it uses multiple senses in the human body - hearing, feeling, and seeing! According to ESPN Sports Science, auditory stimuli reach the brain up to 0.03 seconds faster than visual stimuli. Your brain recognizes sound faster than sight, so when the ball leaves the opponent's racket, the first clue to the ball quality is hearing the contact for more friction (lighter brushing sound) or more force (harder, pounding sound). Next, you see the entire picture of the stroke and incoming ball. Finally, you feel the vibration of the hit, giving you feedback regarding your own ball quality of speed and spin ratio. Table tennis involves all three senses – hearing, feeling, and seeing, and sometimes we jokingly say that it also involves smelling the win and tasting the victory!

Okay, we see that table tennis is great for kids, teens, and young adults, but what about senior citizens? Well, table tennis is recognized by medical practitioners for its benefits on the brain and for the treatment of Alzheimer's and dementia. Studies show that playing table tennis can grow the parts of the brain that are shrinking from these conditions and can activate up to five areas of the brain simultaneously. The results of a recent research study conducted by Bounce Alzheimer's Therapy Foundation (BAT) and a neuroscience team at King's College London showed that playing table tennis regularly can delay the onset of Alzheimer's by as much as five years. Studies also show that the sport improves long-term memory, reduces the need for medication, improves awareness and cognitive thinking, decreases brain deterioration, and enhances motor skills. Considering that there are approximately 5.5 million people living in the United States with either Alzheimer's or a form of dementia, and approximately 44 million people worldwide with these conditions, table tennis has proven to be a huge benefit in helping to fight these diseases.

What about other conditions, such as Parkinson's Disease? According to a recent study (Ken-ichi Inoue, MD, of Fukuoka University in Fukuoka, Japan), Parkinson's patients who played a five-hour table tennis session once a week for six months, experienced significant improvements in speech, handwriting, getting dressed, getting out of bed, and walking. As you can see, table tennis is not only beneficial in developing young minds, but can also be a game-changer in later years to help keep the mind sharp and reduce the struggles of aging and disease. No other sport can challenge the brain quite like table tennis does! Check out the awesome testimonials on the next page!

"I started playing table tennis after having a major brain surgery. Table tennis helped me a lot mentally and physically. My ability to think clearly came back within months."

"At the age of six, I was diagnosed with ADHD and an anxiety disorder. Instead of choosing medication for treatment, I've used table tennis as mental therapy to help with my anxiety. I'm learning to restructure my mental game with coaching techniques from both Samson Dubina and Dora Kurimay. Though I continue to struggle with anxiety, I've learned that instead of viewing my condition as a negative, I've been able to use table tennis as a way to help promote the positive gifts of ADHD such as leadership, athleticism, creativity, and hyper-focus to help excel in the sport."

Chapter 4
Social Aspect

For many years, table tennis has been seen as a social sport that BRINGS PEOPLE TOGETHER! The most notable moment in the history of the sport was Ping Pong Diplomacy. In 1971, at the peak of the Cold War, the US National Table Tennis Team visited Communist China and restored relations between the US and China, which had been in opposition for twenty-two years. This event in history marked a new and lasting relationship between the US and China. Since that time, there have been hundreds of other social situations where table tennis brought people together – Americans, Asians, Europeans, Hispanics, Africans, all coming together to train, compete, and fellowship.

One of the newest social ways that table tennis brings people together today is in the workplace. Many major companies now have table tennis tables in their breakrooms where both the employers and employees can relax, joke around, and enjoy some fun for an hour on lunch break. These companies know that social relationships among co-workers are important and are using table tennis as a means of building those relationships. Google had its first tournament in 2013 with 60 participants. As the interest level has been steadily building, they now have over 600 players participating in their tournaments! According to *Perkbox,* "...table tennis increases concentration and alertness, stimulates brain function, and develops tactical thinking skills" (Pampus 1). Also, for those employees wanting to take it seriously, there are professional coaches that work with company employees on lunch breaks to give advice and also add to the fun social aspect as they are improving! These coaches are available in nearly every city in the US!

For young kids, table tennis is a fun sport to learn together in social groups. Soon after learning the basics, kids start seeing some positive results, including WINNING!!! Being in a healthy and social environment with many others their age can stimulate compete-tiveness, and inspire them to work hard. Even for the "non-competitive kid," this is still a good sport to play in order to socialize with others that are passionate about developing.

So, what about teens? According to *ABC News,* teens spend an average of seven hours and 22 minutes on screen time a day!! This extensive amount of screen time can damage the eyes and reduce the amount of daily time allotted to exercise. Realistically, what exercises can teens do? Can you imagine teenagers going to the gym and walking on treadmills for hours and hours with their friends? Likely not! However, with the social aspect of table tennis, teens can play for many hours late into the night, getting both their exercise and social time!

In recent years, table tennis has also been viewed as a "cool" date-night activity. Your girlfriend is expecting the usual dinner and movie, but why not play table tennis as an exciting alternative? It is active, entertaining, and can be done alone or in a social environment with others! It might just start off as a fun activity to do on weekends, but someday it might progress to a competitive sport for both of you as you train and compete together.

For elite players, table tennis is also social. Being on the US National Team opens up many opportunities in an athlete's career, including invitations to many camps and tournaments. By going to these events, players can get insights from National Team coaches, compete with other team members, and get to know them on a social level. The camps especially are a team-bonding experience for everyone, from the silly moments to the intense drills. Although you may be cut-throat rivals on the court, off the court you're social friends.

Unlike most sports, table tennis brings people of all different countries and nationalities together as a family. Table tennis players have the option to play tournaments both nationally and internationally while meeting friends from all over the world. What other sport can you compete against and become friends with athletes from every continent in the world? What other sport will give you the opportunity to learn about other cultures at such an early age? No wonder table tennis is now the #1 most popular indoor sport in the world and #2 participation sport in the world.

"The community is fantastic. I'm a bit of an introvert (okay fine, an extreme introvert), and I found it very easy to make friends at table tennis clubs. People from all over the world gathered in a place to enjoy a common pleasure. Even when you don't speak the same human language, you can make eye contact, point to a table, and speak the language of table tennis together."

Testimonial by Drew Angell

"Socially, table tennis is a sport that no matter where you travel to, you can find a club to visit and play at, where you will find members that are welcoming and who will always challenge you to play your best. Competing in the Senior National Games has been a highlight and huge challenge for me in table tennis. I always look forward to competing with my doubles partners and seeing and catching up with the many lifelong friends I have made along the way."

Testimonial by Sue Garnier

"My wife and I met through table tennis (she beat me of course). We got to know each other traveling to lessons, tournaments, and clubs. The sport will always be special to us not only because of all the benefits of playing but also because of our relationship and the relationships we have made in the overwhelmingly friendly table tennis community!"

Testimonial by Nathen Eldridge

Chapter 5

Cross-Training

What would you think if we told you that the skills you learn in table tennis can significantly improve your skills in other sports? Unlike most other sports that depend on the weather or season, table tennis can be played year-round. When coaches are scrambling in the winter months to find places to practice seasonal sports such as baseball, football, lacrosse, soccer, tennis, golf, etc., they can utilize local table tennis clubs to work on many of the skills needed in other sports. Let's take a closer look...

Table tennis players must be able to maintain great feeling for the ball, have great timing, great anticipation, and be able to make thousands of quick tactical decisions while mastering their skillset. Studies show that table tennis requires more athleticism than most other sports due to the extensive use of many elements of the human body. The Coaches Association of Canada (CAC) recommends, through the Long-Term Athlete Development (LTAD) program, that children should build and develop nine basic skills, including agility, balance, coordination, catching, throwing, hitting, kicking, running, and jumping. Most sports rarely, if ever, utilize all these skills. Even though kicking may not be directly involved in table tennis, the action of kicking involves balance in the lower body, which is one of the most critical aspects in the sport of table tennis. Therefore, table tennis develops all nine skills essential for child development, as recommended by the LTAD program.

As mentioned in Chapter 3, studies have shown that table tennis improves dynamic visual activity (the ability to see objects when you are moving fast). This is another reason why table tennis can significantly help improve skills in other sports. The reaction time alone in table tennis can help in other sports as table tennis has been proven to be the fastest reaction sport. Developing this quick reaction time within a short distance in table tennis can be a huge benefit in other sports such as volleyball, in which a player must react to a serve from 59 feet away, a batter in baseball reacting to a pitch from 60 feet away, or a tennis player reacting to a ball being launched from 78 feet away. In Major League Baseball, batters have to see the ball, recognize and identify the pitch, determine if it's worth taking a swing at, and then hit the ball - all within a span of three to four-tenths of a second. The reaction time and skills in table tennis are much quicker. Being able to adapt to the revolutions per minute (RPMs) of a ball in most sports and handle the fast spin rate which the ball is traveling is what separates the good athletes from the great ones. An interesting fact is that a table tennis ball can rotate at 8000 RPMs, which is equivalent to the engine of a 2020 Lamborghini Huracán at max power. This rotation rate is significantly higher in comparison to other sports.

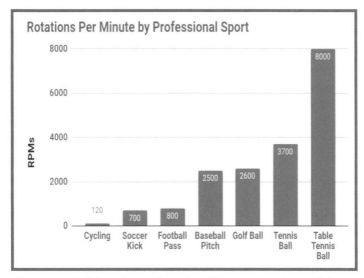

Samson Dubina has played with many elite athletes from other sports (including Golf Pro Matt Kuchar, Indy Racer Josef Newgarden, and Football Star Corey Coleman) that use table tennis as cross-training! Many locker rooms from professional sports are equipped with table tennis tables. Why? Because athletes know that table tennis is the best cross-training sport. They really believe it and their coaches believe it!

Matt Kuchar vs Samson Dubina

So, we have seen the benefits ... Are there risks? Not really! Because it is non-contact, there is low-risk for injury. Because it involves many different movements like looping, counter-looping, blocking, pushing, smashing, chopping, fishing, and lobbing, it is a full-body workout that can help cross-train for any sport. Because it is fun, athletes can do it for hours and hours without getting bored. So, what sport do YOU play? Baseball? Golf? Volleyball? Soccer? Hockey? Play table tennis in the off-season and you too will see the benefits!

Testimonial by Kevin Finn

"Table tennis is a sport like none other—it is rewarding, humbling, and endlessly complex. As a personal trainer, I'm always encouraging people to seek out forms of exercise that don't *feel* like exercise, and table tennis fits the bill perfectly: it's low impact, low risk of injury, can be played year-round, and is great for improving hand-eye coordination. Plus, unlike running, it's not absolute torture! Getting (and staying) fit is not about forcing yourself to exercise, it's about learning to love leading an active life, and table tennis is an incredible way to do just that!"

Testimonial by Chip Coulter

"Table tennis is excellent cross-training for baseball, softball, and golf! Baseball and softball for tracking the incoming ball, and golf for the technical and mental aspects of the game."

Chapter 6
Affordable

C an you afford to play table tennis? What if we told you that you could play competitive table tennis for only $4 per day? Would you believe us? Let's take a closer look...

There are table tennis clubs in nearly every major city in the US. The cost to attend one of these table tennis clubs is around $5-$12/day or $50-100/month membership. You will need to purchase or borrow a racket. Recreational rackets usually cost around $20-$30 and professional rackets are around $75-$200, including both blade and rubber. Professional training balls cost about $1 each with professional Nittaku Premium balls costing around $3 each. It will cost you around $360 for three months of table tennis including purchasing a professional racket, buying balls, and signing up for a 3-month membership. So $360/90 days = $4/day. <u>Only $4 per day!! That IS affordable!</u> Some people play year-round and others join for one season. Equipment is available at both the Samson Dubina Table Tennis Academy as well as through Paddle Palace.

What else is available to help you improve? Group classes, private lessons, leagues, and tournaments. Group classes are usually priced around $10-$15/hour. Private lessons range from $20-$60 for a half-hour lesson. Leagues are usually $10-$15/night or $120 for the full season. Tournaments range from $30-$100, depending on the type of event.

If you want to play at home, you can invite other table tennis players to practice with you or even purchase a table tennis robot. Recreational tables start at $200. Professional tables cost $400+. Getting a quality Power Pong Robot is somewhat expensive, but definitely worth the money. With a setup at home, you can play unlimited for free. With going to the club, you have way more up potential and it can still be done at a reasonable price.

Good News! We offer many resources online including tons of free advice about strokes, footwork, spins, equipment, events, and much much more. For more information, check out SamsonDubina.com, our Facebook page, and YouTube channel.

So, what if you do have some success in table tennis? Does it get more expensive or less expensive? It really depends on your goals and how much you are training, but as you get better, you can win prize money as well. The average large tournament in the US pays around $1,000-$3,000 for first place and $5,000-$20,000 total prize money. The highest paying US tournament in recent years paid $100,000 for first place.

At the elite level, sponsors pay for the equipment needs, including rackets, rubber, shoes, balls, clothes, etc. Some sponsorships also include travel expenses, monthly paychecks, and incentive checks for winning major tournaments. At the elite level, you can make some money, and at the world-class level, you can make over $10,000 per match and $1,000,000 annually from tournament winnings and sponsorships. Samson Dubina is currently sponsored by Nittaku, Paddle Palace, Power Pong, Presper Financial Architects, Aker's Signs, Wil-Cut Engineered Abrasive Solutions, and Red Roof Inn. Each of these sponsors has a different arrangement and supports him differently. So, what is the point? The point is that table tennis can be expensive for the player and parents, but at a higher level, there is payback to the athlete, too. Samson has personally received around $90,000 in tournament winnings and $200,000 from sponsors and received over $220,000 in free equipment in his career. There really are benefits of reaching an elite level.

Chapter 7
Well-Rounded Sport

T able tennis is the most well-rounded sport for the entire family! Kids, teens, adults, and seniors can play alone with a robot, together with a partner, or even in a group for doubles or teams.

Kids can quickly learn to hold the paddle, serve, do some basic footwork, hit simple forehands and backhands, and even experiment with some fancy spins. The game keeps their interest level with new challenges during every rally. Many kids learn hand-eye coordination from bouncing the ball against the wall or dribbling it on the floor. Once kids progress beyond the basic striking skills, they can then appreciate the excitement of learning how to read various spins and impart their own. Kids love seeing how these new skills develop quickly and, of course, they love thrashing their parents, aunts, uncles, and grandparents!

Many adults remember playing table tennis years ago and relish giving the sport another try. They are often pleasantly surprised to see they have maintained some skills and still enjoy the exercise and competition.

Also, table tennis is one of the very few sports that seniors can do at home and also in retirement villages. Seniors love meeting up in the morning for an hour of hitting the ball. Some senior leagues even use larger balls – 55mm instead of the traditional 40mm, which slows the ball down more and gives longer rallies.

Are you going out-of-state to college and don't know anyone? Join the table tennis club! The National Collegiate Table Tennis Association (NCTTA) has division 1, 2, and 3 teams. So, regardless of what level you are at, you can still train and compete at your school, compete against other schools, and even have the chance to play in the NCTTA National Championships! If you are a top-level player, you can get a full or partial college scholarship for table tennis. But even if you haven't achieved national success, you can still train and compete in college events!

People with disabilities can also compete in table tennis. There are para training camps and tournaments worldwide that these players can join. Depending on the level of disability, players are put in different classes. Here are the classes as outlined by the ITTF Coaching Manual and the Paralympic Sports Website:

Sitting Athletes

CLASS	DISABILITY LEVEL
1	Severe restriction of the playing arm, trunk, and lower limbs
2	Moderate restriction of the playing arm and severe restriction of the trunk and lower limbs
3	Normal or mild restriction of the playing arm and moderate restriction of the trunk and lower limbs
4	Normal playing arm, mild restriction of the trunk, severe restriction of the lower limbs
5	Normal playing arm, normal or mild restriction of the trunk, moderate to severe restriction of the lower limbs

Standing Athletes

CLASS	DISABILITY LEVEL
6	Severe restriction of the lower limbs and/or playing arm
7	Severe restriction of the lower limbs or severe restriction of the playing arm
8	Severe restriction of one lower limb or moderate restriction of two lower limbs or moderate to severe restriction of the playing arm
9	Moderate restriction of one lower limb or moderate restriction of the playing arm
10	Mild restriction of one lower limb or mild restriction or the playing arm
11	For players with an intellectual disability

Are you moving to a new city for your dad's work? Look up table tennis clubs in your area. Regardless of who you are or where you live, you are sure to find people who love table tennis. It is a great way of meeting people! Check out the testimonials to hear what others are saying!!!

Testimonial by Chris Jordan

"At 60 years old, newly single, depressed, and out of shape, I discovered table tennis. Not only was it great exercise, but it became a great social outlet as well. No partner was necessary. I'm always around people of all ages and backgrounds. Even as a complete beginner, everyone at the club would play and encourage me to get better. It has been such an important part of my life these last five years. I'm addicted. Why not be addicted to table tennis? I am having fun, getting great exercise, and meeting the most wonderful people!"

Testimonial by Jenson Van Emburgh

"Table tennis has helped me so much in every aspect of life. It has motivated me to be in the best shape physically. Also, it has helped me become mentally stronger along the way!"

Chapter 8
Winning and Learning

I magine this... It's early in the morning, 6:00 A.M. you've studied hours and hours for the huge test today. Then, despite all of your hard work, unfortunately, you did way worse on the test than you wanted. Of course, you're going to feel horrible about yourself. But does this mean you stop trying? Does this mean you give up? *NO!!!* But you might be thinking, "How does this relate to table tennis?"

There will be times when you feel like you just don't have confidence in yourself, when you feel so defeated that you want to just give up. Just like Nelson Mandela stated, "I never lose. I either win or learn from it." The key to improvement is to not be any less motivated by failure. Instead, you should learn from it and come back STRONGER. In order to succeed, you must know what your mistakes were so that you can better yourself next time.

Table tennis can be frustrating because one minor mistake can cost you a match. In this sport, you can learn how to deal with defeat and failure from losing a point, game, or match. Table tennis can help you learn to manage those negative feelings, so when you underperform on that test, you'll know how to pick yourself up. According to the article, *8 Ways Psychologists Say Successful People Achieve Their Goal,* the best athletes become the best because they have a "growth mindset." "Growth mindsets give people the ability to see themselves as capable of change — notably, growth — while fixed mindsets cause people to view themselves as fully realized, or unchanging" (Weller 1). If you have a mindset that is willing to change and learn from failure, then you can be as good as you want to be.

Having confidence in yourself is a huge key to success in many aspects of life, including sports, school, relationships, and the general decisions that you make. Many gain confidence from achieving their goals and knowing that they can do it. According to *activekids.com,* "*...when an athlete wins in an individual sport, they have a strong sense of accomplishment*" (Swanson 1). The feeling of achieving this goal without having to rely on anyone else can increase self-confidence because the athlete has seen themselves do it, and this mindset will help them have more confidence in many life scenarios such as public speaking, test taking, and job interviews. Table tennis is the perfect fit for any kid to build confidence.

Matches are either best 3/5 or 4/7. Each game goes only to 11 points unless you're tied at deuce. With the game having such a short duration, intensity levels can quickly escalate within minutes. Having the ability to keep your head in the game and stay cool is crucial in these situations.

How are you going to handle this pressure? It takes immense focus on each and every ball, which sometimes can be difficult due to the game's blinding speed. By playing table tennis, kids can learn at an early age how to deal with pressure. Even at the lower levels, the game requires an enormous amount of concentration to be able to hit the ball on the table. In pressure situations, they can learn how to stay level-headed and focused. Kids can also learn how to handle their emotions during and after a match. Sometimes a match can be an emotional roller coaster, ranging from the thrilling excitement from a win to the crushing agony from a loss. By gaining experience from playing fun or competitive matches, kids can learn how to deal with their feelings and keep them on the dial. They can learn a unique type of respect for their opponents, especially their rivals, and at the same time keep their cool in the competition.

Picture this: it's match point for you, 10-9 in the final game of the US Olympic Trials. You've been grinding it out in practice your whole life for this moment of making the US Olympic Team.

...All you have to do is win one point to make the team!

...There is a strange silence in the crowd as hundreds of people lean forward to watch intently!

...That feeling of the clench!

...The sound of the ball bouncing!

...The sweat rolling down your forehead!

...And your mind racing 1000 miles per hour is simply exhilarating!

...It is match point for you!

...You whisper to yourself, "Trust, Trust!"

...You step up to the table with confidence!

After a 20-hit rally, you nail the wide corner for the winning shot and are completely overwhelmed by the thrill of the moment! People are congratulating you, you're laughing, talking, and you're enjoying the moment to the fullest! All of your training has paid off, all of the tough early-morning practices, all of the tournament losses, all of the drop-dead fitness sessions, all of the mental training, all paid off in this one final point!

In conclusion, competition is about having the right perspective on winning and losing. As Stephen McCranie said, "The master has failed more times than the beginner has even tried." As an athlete who just won a major title, you know deep down inside that you wouldn't have won that major championship without failing first. Repeating for emphasis ... YOU KNOW DEEP DOWN INSIDE THAT YOU WOULDN'T HAVE WON THAT MAJOR CHAMPIONSHIP WITHOUT FAILING FIRST. Winning and learning ... that's what tournament play is all about!

"Table tennis is a sport which brings me huge mental benefits. It teaches me how to focus, how to be tough, and how to come back from behind. As in real life, you have to cope with many obstacles by forward-thinking, correct your own mistakes with courage, and always try something new."

Testimonial by Julia Mao

Chapter 9
Professional
Approach

D o you want to become an average table tennis player at your local club, a state champion, or an Olympic medalist? With the right training, anything is possible.

If you want to become an Olympian, you should begin no later than 12 years of age. It will take at least 10,000-20,000 quality hours of training under the supervision of a professional coach. Most of the top US players receive about 10-15 hours of private lessons each week as well as group training, leagues, tournaments, and much more.

In addition to spending thousands of hours practicing, professional players also need to learn to handle their emotions and become tournament tough. The average time between points is 8-10 seconds. During that time, the players must be able to process what just happened, remind themselves of their overall strategies, and be able to sift through hundreds of possible combinations as they plan tactics for the next point. For a professional player to reach his peak performance, it isn't just about being physically tough, but also mentally tough. That's what it takes to attain world-class success!

So, what is the benefit of achieving such success? The world's best players make over $1 million US dollars annually from tournament winnings, league winnings, and sponsorships. Also, there are colleges both domestically and around the globe that offer both full and partial table tennis scholarships.

Additionally, you can benefit from the prestigious titles and the experience you have gained along the way. US Olympian Whitney Ping was recently named by Forbes Magazine as one of the top 30 most successful people under age 30. She credits table tennis for her success, adding that table tennis is one of the reasons she was accepted to Stanford and also one of the reasons for her success in the workforce, becoming Vice President of Bain Capital, Director of Hellman & Friedman, and on the board of the US Olympic Committee. Whitney says that it wasn't just the titles but also the experience gained from training and competing at an Olympic level that helped fuel her success.

What kind of experience does a professional player gain? They develop character in a number of different ways. Pro players develop the self-discipline to wake up early and jog three miles before breakfast, to train six hours each day, to go hit the gym at night for some strength and flexibility training, and self-discipline to sleep properly and eat healthily. Pro players learn how to handle controversy. Controversy is a part of everyone's lives ... in college, in a relationship, and in the workplace. You can't avoid controversy, but you can learn how to handle it. Also, these players learn how to negotiate with sponsors and promote products. Pro players learn how to speak to the public through newspapers, TV, and internet interviews. Competing in table tennis at a world-class level isn't just about the title, it is also about the journey and the skills you gain along the way!

Testimonial By Greg Collins

"One aspect of table tennis that is often overlooked is how we conduct ourselves during matches, tournaments, etc., can have an impact on future opportunities. When I graduated from Ohio State with a major in computer science engineering many years ago, it was very difficult to find a job since software engineers weren't high in demand at that time. A hiring manager at a renowned company in the aerospace industry (located in California) knew me from table tennis. He was familiar with my dedication, honesty, and sportsmanship from table tennis, and he hired me with no hesitation. I ultimately retired from that company after working there for 33 years. This was clearly a life-changing event for me that was made possible from table tennis."

Testimonial By Angela Guan

"Table tennis is such an intricate sport and the mental game is so important. For the past ten years, I have been grateful for the mental benefit and lessons that table tennis has taught me. From learning to set a goal of working hard towards it, to staying calm and thinking critically, these are valuable lessons that can be applied to any aspect of table tennis and life. Ultimately, I have learned from Coach Samson that perspective is key in table tennis, life, and beyond!"

Chapter 10

You Are in Control

As you have seen in the preceding chapters, table tennis truly is a sport for all ages, all levels, it is affordable, and it is something that you can do at home or at the local table tennis club. It is a sport that brings people together from all countries, brings people together in the workplace, brings families together, and brings neighbors and friends together. It is a great sport that is healthy for the mind and healthy for the body!

What are you going to choose? Do you want to be an Olympian, the neighborhood champ, or somewhere in-between? The choice is yours! You can choose to play once a month, for just one season, or all year-round. You can choose to buy a basic paddle and show up for drop-in play, or you could buy the latest equipment and take daily lessons. The choice is yours!

So, with a low commitment level, why don't you give it a try? You don't need to stop all other activities in your life, quit your job, drop out of school, and leave your family! You can try it out by stopping in at your local table tennis club for a few games or signing up to take a group class or private lesson.

The good news is that there are table tennis clubs in nearly every city in the US. To find a club, go to www.SamsonDubina.com and click OHIO CLUBS, then click USATT clubs. This will direct you to the entire country of clubs. Major cities like New York City and Los Angeles have 5-10 clubs. Others, like Akron, Ohio, have just one club.

The choice is yours! You have heard of the recreational activity ping pong, but are you ready for the challenge of table tennis? We hope so!

Bonus Chapter
Advice For USATT Clubs

This book was written to help USATT clubs around the country better promote table tennis. The purpose of this book is to give a quick resource to the members of the primary selling points of the sport. This book is also sold in bulk through www.SamsonDubina.com to be used as a giveaway for visitors at your table tennis club. Check out the key points listed below!

Key #1 Be Friendly
When a visitor walks through the door, greet them, introduce yourself, and ask some friendly questions.

Key #2 Start Playing
Make sure that the visitor is playing within the first ten minutes. You should have a table reserved for drop-ins and some loaner rackets available. Within the first ten minutes, your visitor will likely decide if this is the place for him/her.

Key #3 Listen
You need to ask the visitor what he/she likes most about the sport. LISTEN to what he says he likes the most. If the visitor says that he likes to exercise, then turn to Chapter 2 and give him some insightful tips about the physical benefits. If he says that he wants to improve his hand-eye coordination for another sport,

then turn to Chapter 5 and give him some insightful tips about the cross-training benefits. If he says that he wants to meet new friends, then turn to Chapter 4 and talk about the social aspect of the sport. Once you properly understand his motivation for walking through the door, you will then be equipped (with this book) to understand how to convince him to come back!

Key #4 Make the Connection

Introduce the visitor to others! It is very important that he makes a connection with other people at your club, especially players around his age and playing level. There may be one or two very friendly people at your club, so while you should introduce the new player to everyone, in particular make sure to introduce him/her to those members.

Key #5 Get the Visitor Informed

Before leaving, you need to give him a copy of this book - to keep or just to borrow. The main key here is not thinking about the $10 he paid to come for one day but think about the benefit of a LONG-TERM CUSTOMER buying equipment, taking lessons, signing up for tournaments, etc.

Key #6 Invite Him/Her Back

Schedule some time! As he is leaving, make sure that you connect with him. Thank him by name and make sure that you invite him back for a SPECIFIC EVENT! Say something like, "I'll be here early on Saturday, would like you like to come to warm me up at 2pm?" or "Will you be coming to the league on Thursday? It starts at 6:30pm and is a great way to play some other new players." If your visitor marks his calendar and has a plan to come back, he likely will.

Key #7 Reconnect

Reconnect! If you have not seen your visitor for more than one or two weeks, you need to call, text, or e-mail him. Don't do it with a sales pitch. Do it as a friend inviting another friend to come hang out and have fun.

Key #8 Keep Going

The last point to remember is...

Not everyone is going to come back! No matter how amazing your club is, no matter how friendly you are, there are some people who just aren't going to come back. So, if your efforts don't pay off right away, don't be discouraged. Keep going and learn to improve your welcoming skills. As you learn the skill of being friendly and talking about the sport, you will get better and better and your visitors will be more receptive!

Co-Author
Samson Dubina

Coach Samson Dubina was awarded the 2015, 2016, 2017, and 2018 USATT Technology Coach of the Year, and has most recently been named as Technology Coach of the Year from the United States Olympic Committee.

So how did he start??? Samson started table tennis at age 12 in Canton, Ohio, at a local church, then progressed to the Canton Table Tennis Club at the YWCA. Four years later, his game saw huge improvements under the instruction of coach Carl Hardin. He continued sharpening his skills as a training partner for the Canadian Olympic team from 2004-2007. In recent years, Samson has achieved many titles while traveling to Europe, Asia, and throughout North America, competing in nearly 400 tournaments over the last 24 years. Currently, Samson is coaching the top players in the state of Ohio, as well as players around the nation! Samson is happily married to Heather Dubina and they have seven kids, most of whom are now old enough to start playing table tennis and even compete in tournaments.

His favorite Bible verse is 1 Timothy 4:8: "For bodily exercise profits a little, but Godliness is profitable for all things, having promise of the life that now is and of that which is to come." Although Samson promotes the sport of table tennis, his ultimate goal is to share the good news of the Gospel with others and show that table tennis does help in life, but still needs to be kept in perspective with the eternal and better things to come! The biggest game-changer in his life was becoming a Christian, and now his goal is to share the good news of Jesus Christ with others.

Co-Author Jacob Boyd

Jacob Boyd was born and raised in Northeast, Ohio. At a young age, he excelled in a variety of sports, including baseball, football, and basketball. He was eager to play a sport that challenged his mind and ability, involved hard work, individuality, and extreme dedication.

Like many kids, Jacob loved playing recreational ping pong with his dad and grandfather in the basement. At the age of 10, his passion for ping pong led him to the Samson Dubina Table Tennis Academy. It was there that he was introduced to the Olympic sport of Table Tennis where he was welcomed by an entirely new world of friends and family.

Jacob was able to achieve a rating of over 2000 in under three short years. He is currently ranked the #1 male player age 18 and under in Ohio and is the 14th ranked mini-cadet in the United States. With a combination of talented coaches and practice partners, a hard work ethic, his passion for the sport, and the Lord's guidance, Jacob continues to strive toward his goal of representing the US in the Olympic Games.

His favorite Bible verse is Philippians 4:13: "I can do all things through Christ who strengthens me."

Co-Author
Sarah Jalli

At seven years old, Sarah Jalli came to Samson's house and took her first lesson. She played casually for a couple of years. When she competed at the US Nationals, she lost badly to the other girls around her age. With support from her parents, Sarah became more determined than ever, put in the time and effort, and began making rapid progress. Within two years, she captured the Under 11 US Open title without dropping a single game in the event! Fueled by her success, she continued winning many local and national titles, including US National Mini-Cadet Champion, US National Ranking Tournament Champion, and many other titles.

She trains daily at the Samson Dubina Table Tennis Academy, participating in group classes, fitness training sessions, private lessons, leagues, and tournaments. Her goal is to make the 2024 US Olympic Team. She is a great role model as someone who works hard, has a good attitude, and promotes the sport to others.

Her favorite Bible verse is Psalm 16:8: "I have set the Lord always before me; because He is at my right hand I shall not be moved."

Additional Resources

Innovative Products Available Through Samson Dubina Table Tennis Academy

- TT-Flex™
- TT-Flex Pro™
- TT-Serve®

Books and DVDs

- <u>100 Days of Table Tennis</u> Book – By Samson Dubina
  Available at www.SamsonDubina.com

- <u>International Table Tennis Skills</u> DVD – Samson Dubina
  Available at www.SamsonDubina.com

- <u>Professional Table Tennis Coaches Handbook</u> – Larry Hodges
  Available at www.Amazon.com

- <u>Table Tennis Tactics for Thinkers</u> – Larry Hodges
  Available at www.Amazon.com

- <u>Get Your Game Face On</u> – Dora Kurimay
  Available at www.Amazon.com

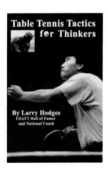
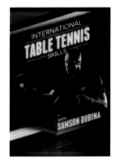
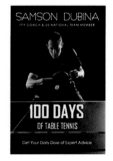

Works Cited

ABC News, ABC News Network, abcnews.go.com/Technology/brain-ping-pong/story?id=12721610

Admin. "The Best Sport For Your Brain." *Game Tables and More*, 28 June 2017, www.gametablesonline.com/blog/best-sport-brain-table-tennis

"All About Table Tennis - Expert Advice, Information, and Top Tips." *AllAboutTableTennis.com*, www.allabouttabletennis.com

"BAT Foundation – Drug-Free Alzheimer's Table Tennis Therapy: Research." *BAT Foundation - Drug-Free Alzheimer's Table Tennis Therapy*, www.batfoundation.com/bat-research

Battley, Andrew. "Is Table Tennis the Future of Alzheimer's Therapy?" *Age UK London Blog*, 31 Mar. 2017, www.ageuklondonblog.org.uk/2017/04/04/table-tennis-alzheimers-therapy

"BENEFITS of Playing Table Tennis." *North Shore Table Tennis Club*, nsttc.ca/benefits-of-playing-table-tennis

Brenkus, John. "ESPN-Sports Science Table Tennis." *ESPN*, 30 June 2013, www.youtube.com/watch?v=_3fTnrUCLCc

Daish, Simon. "Meet Your Dream Women's Team of the 21st Century!" *International Table Tennis Federation*, International Table Tennis Federation, 21 Apr. 2020, www.ittf.com/2020/04/20/meet-dream-womens-team-21st-century

Gordon, Jamie. "Dr. Miriam Stoppard: Why Table Tennis Is Great for the Brain." *Table Tennis England*, 11 May 2017, tabletennisengland.co.uk/news/dr-miriam-stoppard-why-table-tennis-is-great-for-the-brain

"How Ping Pong Can Help Prevent and Treat Alzheimer's Disease." *Ontario Table Tennis*, 6 Dec. 2017, ontariotabletennis.com/news/how-ping-pong-can-help-prevent-and-treat-alzheimers-disease

Why Table Tennis?

Jacobo, Julia. *ABC News*, ABC News Network, 29 Oct. 2019, abcnews.go.com/US/teens-spend-hours-screens-entertainment-day-report/story?id=66607555

Langen, Roger. "Top 10 Most Played Sports." *Pledge Sports*, 8 Apr. 2020, www.pledgesports.org/2017/06/top-10-most-played-sports/

PongBoss and Khaled Say: "Table Tennis and the Brain." *PongBoss*, 9 June 2018, www.pongboss.com/tips/table-tennis-brain

"Science of Table Tennis | The Art of Spin | Episode 1." *Science of Table Tennis | The Art of Spin | Episode 1*, Ultimate Table Tennis, 11 June 2018, www.youtube.com/watch?v=CYqNCQAMFBY

"Science of Table Tennis | The Fitness Quotient | Episode 3." *Science of Table Tennis | The Fitness Quotient | Episode 3*, Ultimate Table Tennis, 11 June 2018, www.youtube.com/watch?v=WzuygbflQVE

"Science Of Table Tennis | The Reflex Factor | Episode 2." *YouTube.com*, Ultimate Table Tennis, 11 June 2018, www.youtube.com/watch?v=clkVMKX3WK0&t=8s

Study Finds Picking up a Pingpong Paddle May Benefit People with Parkinson's, www.aan.com/PressRoom/Home/PressRelease/3773

Swanson, Beth. "The Pros and Cons of Team and Individual Sports for Kids." *active kids*, Active.com, 12 Sept. 2018, www.activekids.com/sports/articles/the-pros-and-cons-of-team-and-individual-sports-for-kids

"Table Tennis Classification & Categories." *International Paralympic Committee*, www.paralympic.org/table-tennis/classification[A1]

Team, Realbuzz. "Top 10 Most Popular Participation Sports In The World." *Realbuzz 5*, 11 Mar. 2019, www.realbuzz.com/articles-interests/sports-activities/article/top-10-most-popular-participation-sports-in-the-world

Weller, Chris. "8 Ways Psychologists Say Successful People Achieve Their Goals." *Business Insider*, Business Insider, 4 Apr. 2017, www.businessinsider.com/how-to-succeed-according-to-psychologists-2017-4

"14 Benefits of Playing Table Tennis (Cerebral, Emotional & Physical Benefits)." *99Sportz*, 18 Jan. 2020, www.99sportz.com/benefits-of-playing-table-tennis

Testimonial

"Table tennis is a sport like none other—it is rewarding, humbling, and endlessly complex. As a personal trainer, I'm always encouraging people to seek out forms of exercise that don't feel like exercise, and table tennis fits the bill perfectly: it's low impact, low risk of injury, can be played year-round, and is great for improving hand-eye coordination. Plus, unlike running, it's not absolute torture! Getting (and staying) fit is not about forcing yourself to exercise, it's about learning to love leading an active life, and table tennis is an incredible way to do just that!"

-Kevin Finn Owner of Walkthrough Fitness

<u>Samson Dubina Table Tennis Academy</u>

Phone: 330-949-9230
E-Mail: tt@SamsonDubina.com
Website: www.SamsonDubina.com
Address: 2262 South Arlington Rd Akron,
            Ohio 44319 USA

Sponsors!
Nittaku, Paddle Palace, Power Pong, Presper Financial Architects, APAPA, Wil-Cut Engineered Abrasive Solutions, Aker's Signs, Red Roof, and the Sports Alliance of Greater Akron.

Made in the USA
Middletown, DE
17 September 2020

18824356R00029